ENCHANTED STORY BOOK

Pablo Gutierrez
Enchanted Story Book

Published by Spines
ISBN: 979-8-89383-383-6

ENCHANTED STORY BOOK
SECOND EDITION

PABLO GUTIERREZ

About the Author

My name is Pablo Gutierrez. I was born in a small town in South Texas. I work for a company that is in the wind turbine business. One of my favorite things to do is read. I can read for hours and get lost in my reading. I would like to share more of my fairy tales and imaginary stories. Some are made up, and some have been around for a long time. And there are some that I have dreamed of in my sleep.

Preface

My books are about enchanted creatures and places and a collection of short stories. In my stories, I want the readers to feel happy and feel their imagination being stirred up. I want them to keep wanting to read more of my stories about dragons, unicorns, sea creatures, and houses that, if they could talk, ask about the American dream and where did we go wrong? Educational and inspiring, giving hope and faith to help them in their life, this is my collection of short stories from A to Z.

Contents

1. Story 1 — 11
2. Story 2 — 17
3. Story 3 — 25
4. Story 4 — 35
5. Story 5 — 43

Story 1
OLD HOUSE

IF THIS OLD HOUSE COULD TALK

Big house, small house, one-floor house or two-floor house. New or old, they all have a story to tell about the people who bought or rented them throughout this house's life.

The first people are the ones who build the new house. They loved their house, and the house loved them. And the years passed, and the house got old, and the house got to know that family well.

It kept that family cool in summer and warm in the winter. Saw the family grow, their happy time and sad times, birthdays and funeral days too.

It even felt their pain when they hurt for any reason. The house felt like a part of the family that lived in it now, all their success and their failures.

That family was growing more members almost every few years. And talk about selling that old house. The house got sad. It wanted to let them know it loved them and could keep caring for them.

But this first family that had lived in it did not know how the house felt about them.

A sign was put up in the front yard that reads house for sale. The house knew the words to say, but it could not talk. That family was never going to know how that house felt about them.

The house knew almost everything about that family. All the holidays, the four seasons, every new member of the family, three boys and one girl and another on the way.

The house was sad; the family was slipping away every day, and they talked about selling that old house.

One day, another family came to see the house. They liked that old house, and for the first time, the house heard the first family say how they were going to miss that old house.

That made the house want to talk more to let them know how much it loved them and would miss them.

When another new family came to see the house for sale, they fell in love with it.

They saw every little corner of the house and loved it inside and the outside, too. It was built on 5 acres and had lots of trees.

The house heard the new family call it this new house they wanted to buy. That new family kept saying how happy they would be in that house.

During all four seasons and all the holidays and birthdays, the house knew what to do for this family, keeping them happy, and the house would be happy, too.

How many houses get abandoned and broken by families that don't know what a house should be?

A place for safety, a shelter and a place to call home. That house had a lot to say to the two families that the house's Job was to love and take care of any family that got to live in it and always make them happy.

Now you know what it means when you hear that almost all the houses make some kind of noise, like the pipes and windows, doors and sometimes the walls.

But we know the house is trying to talk to let Someone know that It needs some tender loving maintenance or that it is lonely or maybe just to let us know it wants to be home.

You see, it's the same as anything. A house has to be the right size for any family when the family is young and a first-time home buyer.

They need a small house, two bedrooms, one bath, a kitchen, and a living room, just the right size for dad and mom, and one baby boy or girl, but some people don't see it that way. They see the price. If the price is right, they want to buy it for a family of four, knowing the house is one room short.

In the long run, it pays to make the right choice or decision, but you know what they say: plan for your future. Don't make a mistake in this life with something that costs way more than just some of what we call toys.

Good advice is always helpful when buying a house, but try to get professional advice. You don't want to end up telling yourself that no one told you when it's already signed, sealed and done. You see, a professional does not just want to sell; they tell you all that comes in when buying a house.

FOR
SALE

Story 2
TWO ROADS

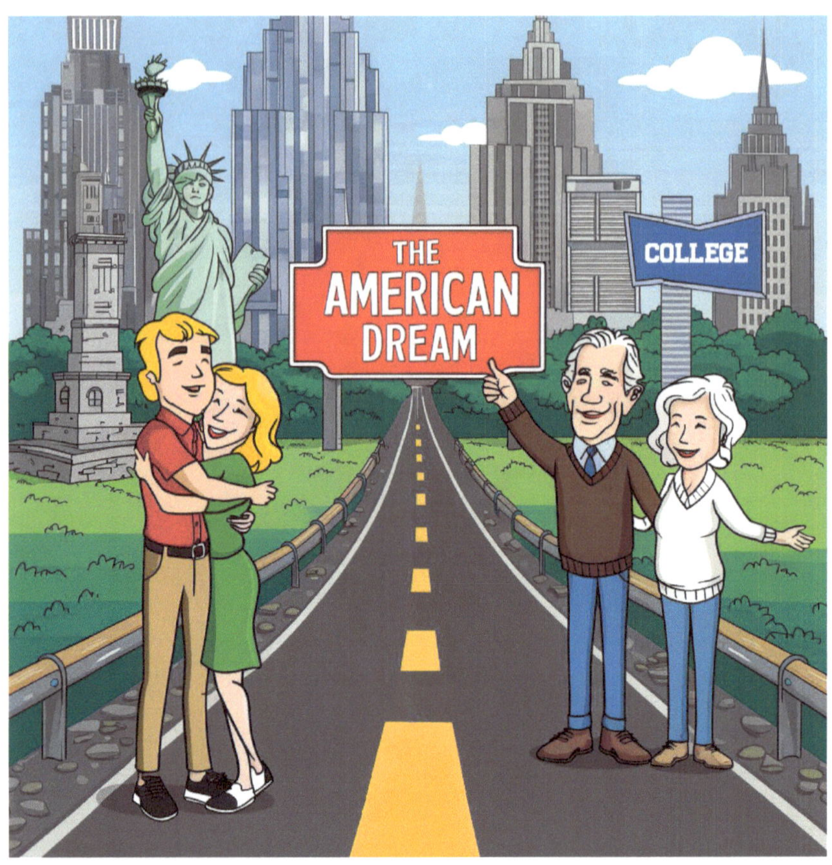

This story is about two roads that every male and female has to take in this life.

It all starts like this: there is a saying at the right place at the right time for the opportunity. Well, this is born in the right family at the right time. The first road, more people just remember, is as far back as Grandma and Grandpa, and some do not even remember that part of their early life.

If you were born into a good family, the ones that always had the American dream in their minds and hearts.

The ones that dad and mom both had jobs and grandparents that made sure all their grandchildren finished school and went to college.

The ones who were taught the right road that leads to a successful American dream in their life ever since they were young.

A family that wants every member of the family to be successful. Every person born, since a baby boy or girl, is taught well, good manners to respect, to love and to be successful.

They are taught how every person has a part in this life and how every generation has kept on the same road to succeed.

Since the early years of America, almost every family has wanted the American dream.

That all their generations did something for their country. First, get a good education. Next, decide what career you want, start your own business, serve your country in the military, get married, buy stocks, buy a house, and start a family.

That sounds easy, but that road is hard to stay on. The family has to be brave and have a strong will and one that doesn't know how to quit.

And some good generations of knowledge to back them. Some families have mastered that road that leads to a successful life in America.

There is a saying that money can't buy you love, but it can buy you a good life.

Imagine being born in one of these families that have these maps to the successful road.

To enjoy buying a house and a car and starting your own business on every birthday, every holiday, and on vacation.

Sounds too good to be true, but listening to good advice pays off. It sounds like a good road.

There are so many roads in this life story. This is the second road.

This road is similar to the first road, but the opposite family has heard about the American dream but does not have the map for that road.

Unfortunately, in this time of age, every person, male or female, wants to be famous and rich. They follow their own dream.

When they are born, it is quiet in the hospital. But when they come home, their little minds are distracted and confused by all the noise. Local music, people shouting, and dogs barking the TV too loud. To start a new life distracted and confused is not going to lead anyone to a good road.

Well, Grandma and Grandpa live so far away. They are still looking for the right road. They once heard when they were young.

Dad has a good job, but he is gone most of the time; Ma has to do two jobs: mother's job and father's job. The children have to grow up on their own.

Dream of a successful life with no map. No generation looks back for guidance.

Almost going through life in darkness with no clue of what life to choose.

It's nobody's fault. It's just that a dream is not a successful dream. There is the saying tell me who you hang around with, and I will tell you who you are.

Good guidance, a good mentor, and good advice are the battcrics for a good listener with a strong will to light the darkness in the mind so he or she can find the right road.

There is a saying that people want a better world, but what makes a better world? People are the ones who make this world better. They take care of everything in it.

What makes people better is knowledge, wisdom, and education, which are important. It helps you clean the bad education. The one that is heavy and doesn't let your mind move forward.

But good pure education is light and lets your mind think and be hungry for more.

Yes, they say that you or anybody can do whatever you put your mind to, whatever you want to be or want to achieve.

But in that saying, they leave out all the steps to get there. We all want to enjoy life with houses and cars, start a business, buy stock and serve our country.

Enjoy some vacations and all the holidays, but some of us will never. Why did they stop dreaming? For the young that lost their way, all they need is to tune up their mind to the right thinking and the right people, and they will start moving towards the right road.

And for us older people, we can start cleaning the house after years of not cleaning, all the bad stuff out of our minds and letting only positive thinking. In so we can help our young loved ones who are still lost on the wrong road and bring them back to the right Road.

Yes, any person can change their situation just by thinking positively when they feel trapped in a box or on a merry-go-round, but only that person who feels lost, confused, and sometimes sick. If there is no hope or escape for you in this life, remember good manners, respect, love, and positive thinking. The more positive things you add to yourself, the faster success comes to you. It's like, just think like this: if you want oranges, plant a banana tree, and you will get oranges or what? Bananas?

Whatever have you stuck, think the opposite and throw all the negative thinking out of your mind. Do it for yourself, help yourself; we are superhumans but don't know it. Think smart, think happy, think love, think successful. Only you can change your world.

THE
AMERICAN
DREAM
COLLEGE
DEAD END

Story 3
TWO KINGS

AT WAR

Way back in ancient times, castles and enchanted mythical creatures of all kinds.

Lived a king with the Bloodline in his veins of the Ancient Dragon layer. There also lived another king, but this king was a mythical Dragon creature leader of all the Dragons with special powers. Not only could he breathe out fire, but he could also make himself invisible and speak ten languages.

He, like all the other dragons, loved to fly; his Bloodline was enchanted and royal when he was born for the first time on this earth that night, and two moons were shining the night.

The only Dragon born that night of the two moons. As far as any dragon was found, they heard of the baby Dragon that was born on the Night of the two moons.

Every Dragon knew that Baby Dragon was going to be a special and powerful king. But what the Dragons did not know was that on the same night, another baby was born, the Night of the Two Moons.

A human King destined to conquer any enemy and any Kingdom. A superhuman carrying six Bloodlines of Kings in his veins.

That time was a magical and enchanted time. Every mythical creature that existed lived in abundance in the forest, rivers, lakes, oceans, mountains, and some in caves.

This earth was new. It nourished everything and gave food in abundance for all living humans, animals and creatures.

Just imagine the places where the enchanted creatures would hang out to eat and drink water, such as a beautiful forest and waterfall that leads to a blue water-running river.

All the places, only the ones with wings, could be so beautiful. A big green forest, as far as the eyes could see, with beautiful mountains and snow on top.

Enchanted creatures and places are a magical time indeed. As time passed, the dragons and the humans became more populated, and that became a big problem.

Every encounter was a dragon killed or, worse, a human, and it got so bad. The people cried out to the king for help. The king has a special army to fight the dragon.

The army was trained to fight a creature that could fly, breathe fire, and have an armored body.

That time was a time of abundance, but the Dragons were eating cows and horses, all kinds of livestock and humans too.

So, the king sent out his Army to kill as many Dragons as they could. Three thousand on horse and Wagons with big arrows weapons.

When they attacked the Dragons, they found out the Dragons had a secret weapon that could turn invisible at will.

And they had the biggest, most powerful Dragon, the king of all the Dragons, fighting the human Army too.

This dragon was a unique and beautiful dragon that only he could change colors from red to green, blue to gold, orange, or any color he wanted.

The fight lasted all day. At the end of that day, the human army was defeated by the dragons, and two thousand men were wiped out.

When the news got back to the king, he was shocked at how many men he had lost when he was told of the special Dragon that could change colors and had what looked like a king's Crown on his head, the most powerful Dragon of them all.

He started looking for information on that dragon and if anything had been written about it before his time.

In a village about 300 miles away near the Enchanted Forest near a big mountain where, on the night of the two moons, a baby dragon was born.

This village had befriended the Dragons before everything got out of control with the humans.

The father and mother of the Dragon born on the Night of the two moons could speak the human language.

That people knew about the baby Dragon king. They also knew about the baby human King who was born on the Night of the Two Moons. They knew the two kings were the same age.

The Dragon King called all the Dragons to the mountain where he was born, the mountain near the enchanted forest.

On the top of the mountain was the entrance to the cave where he lived. He talked to all the Dragons in the Dragon language. The other nine were for humans, enchanted creatures, the forest, lakes and the ocean.

Yes, he was special, the only one like that royal and enchanted bloodline. After the human army had lost, the people were afraid, and they kept asking the king for protection.

The people didn't want to work the fields and the livestock. The king sent out men to all the surrounding villages and big cities for help with the Dragons.

When they came to the village in the enchanted forest, they were told the old stories of the Dragons.

But kept the secret of the king of the two moons. The elders, the old people of the village, were the dragon's friends.

The men were told to go back and bring the king back to them so they could tell him their secret.

When the men got back and told the good news to the king, he was thankful and happy that someone knew something about the Dragons.

In three days, he was ready for the long journey to the village. He arrived by night and was told to rest, and in the morning, he would be told everything he needed to know about the Dragons.

When morning came, the king was taken to the elders at the foot of the mountain, where there was another entrance.

When the elder used to meet with the parents and grandparents of this dragon king, one of the first things they told the human king was that the Dragon king was the same age as him.

And that he was also born the same Night of the two moons and that he too was an ancient Royal bloodline.

A Royal Bloodline is like a human king, and they know that the only way he can be stopped is not to be killed.

By a sword made with a special iron that could only be found in that mountain where the Dragon was born.

That iron was the only metal that could penetrate a dragon's armored body, and the only one that could fight the Dragon and do that was another born on the Night of the Two Moons and Royal Bloodline like him.

That would stop all the other Dragons. It will not kill the Dragon King but put him in a deep sleep and turn him into a rock until another Royal Bloodline comes and pulls out that sword.

No king; the other Dragons must go far away from the humans and live by themselves.

But the human king was told that he had to fight the Dragon in the mountain home. So before they sent the human King back to his Kingdom, they gave him a piece of iron to make the special sword.

Those elders in that village used to train Dragon Slayers from all the surrounding kingdoms.

They told the human King what to use to make a special shield for fire.

He was told to be back there in seven days for the Night of the Moon, and the Dragon would be there, too.

When the night of the Moon came that night, the Dragon king was put to sleep until another king with Royal Bloodline came and Pulls out the sword from that rock.

The year passed, the human King got old and died, and the Dragon still flew over that country but was too afraid to stop.

Those village elders, one by one, died, but scrolls were kept of the stories of the two Kings Born on the Night of the Two Moons.

A special scroll with instructions and the secret of the stone was kept in a safe place with the sword.

Until another Royal Bloodline worthy and enchanted as the Dragon in the Rock.

Story 4
THE LOST DAGGER

The Lost Dagger was about a dream I had, and it goes like this.

There was a man traveling by airplane from America to Africa.

The plane was supposed to land in the capital of Africa, but it never made it there.

The plane was shut down by some gorilla army wanting something that the plane brought back from the States.

The plane crashed into a lake in the jungle. Some survived the crash. One man knew how dangerous the jungle was.

Went down to the luggage and crate compartment to look for anything to use as a weapon. What the survivors did not know was that the impact had attracted the predators in the water and on land.

They started hearing people screaming. He rushed to go help, but he could not believe his eyes. Those people were being eaten alive.

Some kind of unknown species of what looked like giant snakes. Every living animal in that water was being eaten. The impact of the plane crash woke up some ancient species of snakes hungry. The man hurried to find some kind of weapon. All he found was a dagger in a broken crate.

The crate was labeled from the museum U.S.A. He thought it was just an old knife. It came in some kind of an old sheath belt to put around your waist.

It looked like something unique made by a special, talented craftsman made for a king or for some kind of person with Royal blood in him. As soon as he got ready to walk off the crashed plane, one of those snakes got a hold of him.

The snake wrapped itself around the man's body and stared him in the eyes, ready to make that man his next meal. That snake started eating the man's head first. When it got to that man's waste, it let go of the wrap it had around the man's legs.

The snake stretched the man on the ground so it could put all the man's body in it with his legs still out of the snake's mouth; he remembered he had the dagger, and his hands were free inside the snake.

He grabbed the dagger. As soon as the dagger touched the head of the snake, it cut like a laser, tearing the head and body as far as his hand could reach. Opening it like a zipper, the man grasped for air, not knowing what had just happened to him, but he was alive.

Some villagers had been looking for the crash too and found the man still in the snake, and the man was taken to their village.

These people helped him with his wounds. He was there for two days because the gorilla army found the plane crash, but it was not what they were looking for. They traced the foot prints in the village and took the man to their chief deeper into the jungle.

When they arrived at their chief camp, the chief got very angry when he was told they found nothing in the crash. He wanted to see the man that survived the crash.

The villager that found the man told the gorilla's army that only one man was found in that plane crash, and one of those snakes had tried to eat him, and they found the snake dead. Someone had cut open the snake.

From the head to the back of the neck, it is about 3 to 4 feet cut. When they helped the man, he was unconscious, so they took him to their village. They also said he did not have any weapons at all on him.

When they found him in the crash, they told the chief he didn't know anything. The chief started yelling for his gorilla's army commander to get rid of him, that he was useless to him.

He asked the man if that snake didn't eat him. The one he had captured in the river was bigger, and they had it in a big hole where they were going to throw him. That man didn't talk much, never said anything about the dagger he had around his waist.

When they got to the opening of that hole, they saw that the snake was much bigger, but for some unknown reason, he was not afraid of that snake, and while the man was still looking down in that hole, he was pushed in by the Gorilla commander, and they left as fast as they could. They were all afraid of that giant snake.

They knew that anything that fell in would not come out. But the man, when he was pushed, he grabbed the dagger before he hit the ground.

The snake rushed to catch him. It was kept hungry, but he met it with the dagger, and as soon as it touched the snake, it cut straight through the middle of the snake, cutting it into two parts. Still in that hole, he could hear some helicopters flying in the area. One of the pilots saw him, landed the helicopter, and rescued him.

When they rescued this man, he told them about the other survivors and how they had been eaten by those snakes. He also told them how the same gorilla army was after something in that airplane but found nothing in the crash. They took him to a hotel to get washed up and got him some new clothes before he was taken to the hospital to get checked for any injuries.

Because he had a busy day ahead, answering all the questions about how he survived the crash and the jungle and how he ended up.

In that hole with that giant snake, when he answered all their questions and finished with his story, he asked them what they were looking for from that plane.

He was told that there was a crate that had a dagger that was sacred and ancient, made with Iron that came from a meteor rock that fell in that Jungle a long time ago, and a special craftsman was used to make that dagger that had rubies, diamond and gold and silver the iron had some kind of power that could cut through anything like a laser and help the person that wore it.

It even would and could become invisible. The more he heard about the Dagger, the more he remembered how he used it with the first snake and when the villager and the gorilla's army could never see the dagger.

And the second giant snake, the Dagger, split into two pieces. He was happy and grateful, but he knew that Dagger belonged to somebody else. So he told them that he had made it out alive from that Jungle.

And he had experienced its power. The people from Africa were happy to have their Dagger in their possession again. It had helped make Africa a country with its power.

In my dream, I never found out who the dagger was made for, which left me thinking about how old that dagger was. Was it made for a king or for some kind of person with Royal Blood in him? Maybe it even passed through Tarzan's hands?

One thing for sure is that that person had to wear the belt to activate its power and make that person wearing it like a superhuman. This is another story I dreamed of putting in writing, and I bring it to life. I hope you like it.

Story 5
TIME

This story is about time; everything born on this earth has a time, like us humans and animals and everything living around us. Yes, it looks like everything is born with a time to do what it was born to do.

But some, like us humans, don't or can't understand time and its importance. We do have some excuses for our time, and that's when we are babies, and we can't really do too much with time, but we can sleep or cry. For sure, there is a lot of laughter, but as soon as we start putting our feet in and out of the circle of life. Like for some, a daycare and for other schools, anything that has to do with leaving the safety of your home to the outside world.

That's when we really meet time, or to say every one of us was born with a time. Time to get up in the morning, time for breakfast, time for school or time for work. Yes, there is a time for everything.

But some of us still have a saying we have all the time in the world. When you understand time, that's saying it is scary and your worst enemy because we cannot see the future.

It's very important to learn about time, not just about your watch time or clock time. No, this is not a class like in school. I mean, looking at how much we can do in one day's time. Our mind and body should be able to help and work on our behalf.

I know it sounds strange, but it's not just a story about time. To help some of us without knowing or without seeing, we waste a lot of time in our lives.

We all were given some advice one time in our lives about not wasting our time doing nothing. Well, some of us did hear that, but the way it came in one ear, it went out the other faster.

We all, not just some of us, are born equipped to learn, to think, to understand, and to learn knowledge. Yes, but all of them need us to put time into them. But the saying again is that we get all the time in the world.

Yes, some do, and some don't put time into learning and thinking good and right things to understand and, yes, to know knowledge. The thing that we all need to be healthy and successful in our lifetime is.

It would be good if we all knew how much time we had in our life, 25, 50, or 75, and maybe 100 years. And we could take giant steps and catch up with all the rest of the people who did not lose today's dream or that couch potato thing and did not waste their time.

One thing I remember for sure is the time when I was still a youngster and had lived in my dad's house with my siblings since I was the youngest. I had what is called a free ride. My chores list was small, and it was a happy and fun time.

No one prepared me for what was coming. My dad tried but failed. Yes, I heard that saying from one of these so-called couch potatoes about all the time in the world. They sound smart with their talk as if it's easier to have fun than to think and strain your mind.

But good, there are a lot of things we have built in us to succeed, like persistence and someone's persistence on me and guess what? It worked.

I hope this story helps someone who has heard that saying and can't shake it off. And as long you can read these life signs: left turn, right turn, and do not enter or, worst, dead end, you will be fine with your Time.

The question is what we are going to do with this magical and enchanted time we were born with.

This power is to live our lives the right way or the wrong way. What a big thing in our life is this so-called time. So many people don't understand that time is not meant to be wasted but to be used to build your life the best way possible.

What a big earth, and everything in it has time to do what it was born to do with its time. What could be a beautiful thing or a very ugly thing, but it's up to me, you, and everyone in this big, beautiful world, and I know the best thing to do is to make time the best thing in our life.

SCHOOL